Other Works by Jackson Arthur

Collections

A Splash of Crimson: Strange and Scary Stories

Cellar Door: Short Horror Stories

They Come When They Are Called: Supernatural Stories

Orange Eyes Watching

An Ohio Grassman Story

Jackson Arthur

"Every crag and gnarled tree and lonely valley has its own strange and graceful legend attached to it."

- Douglas Hyde

1

The sun was already touching the horizon when we finally turned onto the dirt road leading to the cabin. The tires of my car made a dull *thump thump*, as they left the asphalt highway for the narrow country path, and the sound was like a long, comforting exhale. My shoulders relaxed. And I could feel my tired mind awakening, as the fatigue of a long semester was put on pause for one whole week.

"Are you sure?" I asked, glancing sideways at my girlfriend Penny. Bright rays from the setting sun poured unadulterated through the windshield, transforming her blonde hair into an even lighter shade of gold. Her eyes were glowing, like the bluest ocean beneath the fading light of dusk. "We could always turn around."

"Stop asking me that," she replied without meeting my brief gaze. "If you don't want to be here, then pull over and get out. I'll be just fine without you, all alone in the belly of raw nature. Have fun walking, though. If you start now, you might make it back to the campus in a couple days." She tried to sound serious, but the dimple of her left cheek deepened, giving her away.

"You would just take my car and stay at my uncle's cabin without me?"

"Your car," Penny replied. "Your uncle's cabin. You. You. Not everything is about you, you know. And yes, yes I would. I might even find some burly woodsman, with a broad chest, strong arms, and a face that hasn't seen a razor in over 10 years. We could settle down and have three or four kids. And we would run barefoot through the forest, hunting and foraging like the free folk that we are."

"Hunting and foraging?" I asked, stifling back a chuckle. "We are in Ohio. In 2022. Not the hollers of 1920s West Virginia."

"Does 1920s West Virginia have Starbucks?"

"I doubt it."

"I'm out," she said, throwing up her hands in defeat. "I'd die without my white iced chocolate mocha with dark chocolate drizzle. Without espresso, my heart would literally stop beating."

"You flipped on that pretty fast," I insisted. "Are you sure that you're okay with this, though? If you would rather spend spring break getting toasted on a beach, I'd understand. Where were Mac and Jillian going, again? The Outer Banks?"

"Do you want to go to the Outer Banks? Because it kinda sounds like you might."

"Not really," I replied. "I sunburn too easily. And I can't drink in the heat. It makes me sick."

"Shut up, then. Why would I want to spend a week on a crowded beach, when I could spend a week all alone in the woods with you? Easy choice, if you ask me."

"Okay," I said. "But if some brawny woodcutter from the 1920s comes along, at least let me call an Uber. We are kinda far from Columbus. And I haven't been keeping up with my cardio. I probably wouldn't make it past Akron without dying from exhaustion."

"I promise to consider it," Penny replied. "But I don't think they had Uber in the 1920s. Just saying. Time travel is complicated."

Thick pines crowded the road, blocking most of the waning sunlight from reaching us. As we drove deeper into the woods, deeper into the shadows, I felt the temperature dropping. A chill was setting in, and it would get even colder after the sun was gone. It was a welcome change, though, after the abnormally hot April day. And it would be the perfect night to sit around a warm, crackling fire.

I reached out and flicked off the car's AC before rolling down my window, allowing the sharp aroma of pine, oak, hearty soil, and newly grown flowers to pour in. A cacophony of rowdy insects and birds entered the car, as well. The chirping and tweeting was a far cry from the honking horns and blaring sirens of the city we left behind.

Penny put her window down, too, and then stuck her arm through the opening. Placing the palm of her hand against the force of the wind, she pushed back, a youthful grin forming on her lips. From the corner of my eye, I watched her, picturing a much younger Penny doing the same thing, while riding somewhere with her parents. Most kids did it, as if they could defy the will of nature with a single, outstretched hand. Nature usually won, in my experience, and the kid's hand was always driven backward.

"Watch out!" Penny suddenly shrieked.

My foot immediately slammed down onto the brake, forcing the car into a brief slide. Rushing blood pounded in my ears and it was difficult to catch my breath. My attention had lingered a little too long on Penny and I nearly plowed into a family of deer casually crossing the dirt road. The buck, a massive animal with an impressive rack, stopped a couple of inches from our car's front bumper and intensely eyed us. He refused to move or look away until his doe and faun were safely across. With a stern snort, the buck puffed out his nostrils and shook his head, as if reminding us whose world we were in. After a second, less dramatic snort, the buck moved on, disappearing into the woods.

"Are you okay?" I asked, my heart finally slowing.

"I think I found my broad-chested woodsman," she replied. "Too bad he is already taken. I guess I'm stuck with you."

"I'm honored. Maybe the wife and kid will end up in some hunter's freezer. Your man will be free to see other people, then."

"Fingers crossed," Penny said. "Can we go now? I need to pee."

I laughed and got the car moving again.

2

A few minutes later, we pulled to a stop outside my uncle's cabin, and I felt a long-held tension release in the back of my neck. Festering doubts and burrowing fears have been plaguing me during our long drive east, and I was happy for the relief. Having never been to the cabin, I wasn't sure what to expect. My uncle was far from a careless or messy man, and the home he regularly lived in was always immaculate. So, I knew that my fears were most likely misplaced. Yet, I couldn't keep from picturing the cabin as an abandoned dump, a pile of rotting logs and planks infested by rodents or other woodland creatures.

Thankfully, that wasn't the case. The cabin was a modern, single-story paradise, a secret oasis perfectly tucked away into the woods, hidden from outsiders by tall, hefty pine trees. Both the exterior and the wraparound porch were covered in a layer of glossy, dark cherry varnish, which caught the few remaining shards of sunlight. A wall of firewood lined a wide stone firepit on the right, each log and rock perfectly placed.

Even the trees appeared to be pruned and manicured into a nearly precise circular parameter around the cabin. My uncle must have hired someone to constantly maintain the property in his absence because nothing was out of place. There wasn't a single fallen branch or misplaced leaf to be seen.

"And you said your uncle never comes here anymore?" Penny asked.

"That's what he said," I replied.

"Why the hell not? This place is beautiful. You might have to drag me out of here in a week. Is a week long enough to establish squatter's rights? Asking for a friend."

"Not sure. Let's give it a shot."

"This place must have cost a fortune. What does your uncle do for a living?"

"Makes a shit load of money."

"Maybe you should change your major to that," she half-joked. "And then you could buy me a couple of these for my birthday next year."

"Keep dreaming."

Without another word, we climbed from the car and pulled our suitcases and duffle bags from the trunk. Our first load in hand, we marched to the front of the cabin, where I unlocked the door using the key my uncle had given me. The inside was just as clean, void of any dust or dirt or nesting rodents. We both made a beeline through the moderately furnished living room area to the single bedroom at the back, ready to discard our heavy burden.

"Why don't you bring in the rest of our stuff," Penny began, "while I get the fire going. Well, after I pee, anyway."

"The rest of *our* stuff?" I asked, pointing to the small black suitcase and OSU duffle bag lying by the foot of the queen-sized bed. "All of *my* stuff is right there. The rest of that other crap outside is all yours, babydoll. I think you might really be trying to live here."

"Thank you, sweety," she replied. "Love you, too. Maybe bring me a glass of wine when you're done?"

"Sure thing," I said sarcastically. "Moscato or Sangria?"

"Yes, please."

By the time that I was done being Penny's pack mule, she had a hearty pile of logs burning in the stone pit. The sun was gone and the flames cast beautiful dancing light against the dark of the night. Wonderful heat rose from the blossoming fire, drawing my chilled body in like a wandering moth.

After handing Penny a tall glass of rosy wine, I was finally able to sit down and settle in. Penny was curled up in a bulky patio chair close to the fire, so I grabbed another one and slid it over next to her. With a long sigh, I fell into the chair's thick blue cushions as if they were the softest clouds in heaven.

We both took a long, simultaneous chug of wine and our taste buds ravenously enjoyed the fruity alcoholic beverage.

"I'm glad that you forced me to come here," Penny said, extending her wine glass toward me. "Cheers."

"Cheers."

First, our glasses came together in a dull *clink*, and then our mouths found one another, as well. Her lips were nearly as warm as the fire and just as pleasing. A snapping branch and rustling bush suddenly interrupted our embrace. Whatever it was, it was close. Too close. More sounds of movement came from the woods, from somewhere to our left. Something was coming toward us. And it was moving fast. The serenading insects and singing night birds had silenced, as if the forest was holding its breath.

"What is that?" Penny asked, pulling away from me.

"I don't know," I replied, my muscles tensing. Squinting my eyes, I attempted to see into the darkness between the trees, but the black was too dense. "I don't know."

Without warning, three rushing figures emerged from the darkness, sprinting in our direction, like specters appearing from thin air. As they crashed through the treeline and into the light of the fire, I instantly recognized the three deer from the road. Something had changed, though, because they were no longer moving in a casual, unhurried manner. They were panicked, their black eyes wide and filled with wild terror. The buck emitted frightened grunts and snorts, his massive hooves kicking up dirt, grass, and loose stones as he plowed across my uncle's property.

"What the hell?" Penny exclaimed and then grabbed hold of my arm.

I couldn't respond. Even after the hysterical trio had vanished back into the trees, I found it hard to speak. The whole scene had been surreal and off-putting.

"Was something chasing them?" Penny asked as if reading my mind. "Are there black bears around here?"

"I don't think so," I replied. "Maybe small ones."

"What do bears eat?" she asked.

"I don't know," I admitted. "Berries. Insects. Twigs. Maybe fish or squirrels."

"Deer? People?"

"I don't think so."

"Does your uncle keep a gun in his cabin?" Penny asked. "A big one with lots of bullets?"

"Maybe," I answered. "But I know for sure that he has a hot tub in the master bathroom. Are you ready to go inside?"

"What about the fire?"

"It'll be fine," I replied. "I'll check on it later."

We stood up and cautiously walked toward the cabin, my heart still beating fast in my chest. I listened to the woods, waiting for the insects and birds to reignite their whimsical songs. But they never did. The forest remained uncomfortably silent.

3

The combination of a long drive, fruity wine, and a soothing hot tub relaxed us enough that we retired to bed a little earlier than we usually would. Penny was planning a big day. And her schedule of fun-filled events, which included a pancake breakfast, hiking, and lots of day drinking, involved waking up with the sun. Since when did spring break consist of getting up super early in the morning? I wasn't entirely thrilled, but I didn't argue, either. It was a small price to pay.

As Penny's soft, cute snores filled the bedroom, I glared silently at the ceiling, struggling to fall asleep. Something was still nagging at me, making it difficult to shut down my thoughts. Images of the three deer continued flashing through my head, particularly the buck. The wide black eyes and terrified grunts weren't what kept me from sleeping. There was something else bothering me, something that I hadn't told Penny, because I knew that it would further scare her.

Taking a deep breath, I tried to push the mental image away, but it only became clearer. I saw the broad side of the buck darting by me, its tan fur split open in five long, bloody gashes, as if five jagged claws had sunk into its hide and tried to grab hold.

Had it really been a bear? I couldn't be sure. Maybe. But the bloody marks didn't match what little I knew about bear claws. They were too spread out, as if made by a large…human hand.

Bang!

The unexpected sound of something large smacking against the side of the cabin jolted me upright in bed.

Bang!

Was that a rock? Was someone throwing rocks at the cabin?

I glanced over at Penny, but her consistent snoring told me that she didn't hear it. The woman could sleep through a hurricane.

Another stone stuck the roof with an empty *clack,* and then skipped down the slight incline to the ground. *Clack. Clack. Clack.* Was it just acorns or something falling from the trees? But there weren't any branches extending overtop the cabin.

Something suddenly drew my attention toward the window. A pair of large eyes peered in at me, two orange orbs like lanterns in the darkness. Instinctively, I turned my head away and then counted to three before looking back. They were gone. The window was black and empty. I forced a scream back down my throat and rationalized it all away. My anxiety was causing me to see things that weren't there. That was all. Growing up in places like Columbus, I wasn't accustomed to the quiet and isolation of the woods, and my imagination was in overdrive.

Cautiously, I slipped from the bed, walked to the window, and pulled shut the brown curtains.

4

Orange eyes followed me into my dreams, the glowing orbs watching me from the corners of every nightmare. What few dreams I had, anyway. I spent most of the night tossing and turning, my mind plagued by paranoia, my body plagued by uncomfortable cold sweats. Whenever I did manage to fall into a semi-deep sleep, the sounds of something hard smacking into the cabin woke me.

Not Penny, though. She slept like a log and then hit the ground running the next morning, surprising me with breakfast in bed. The pancakes were fluffy. The coffee was full of Splenda and caramel creamer. And the slices of bacon were perfectly chewy. Somehow, I slept through both the smell of sizzling pork and my girlfriend's off-tune singing. She always belted Ariana Grande songs whenever she cooked.

All I wanted to do after eating was lounge around in bed, but Penny was bright and shiny and ready to move. Luckily, I was able to stall the day drinking until after our morning hike. Alcohol would make me even more tired, and stumbling drunkenly, half-asleep through the Cuyahoga Valley didn't sound too safe.

"It might rain," I mentioned as we exited the cabin and into the brisk air. "The clouds are looking a little sad. They might cry."

"Both of our umbrellas are packed," she replied, motioning to the large pink camo backpack she was hauling. "And so is your green parka. Maybe you should just put it on now."

"It'll be too hot once it warms up. My hoodie will work."

"Which way are we going?" she asked.

"Behind the cabin is a four-wheeler trail that we can use," I answered. "It might be a little overgrown, my uncle said, but we should still be able to follow it pretty easily."

"Your uncle has a four-wheeler?" Her eyes lit up. "Where is it? Can we drive it around?"

"It'd be nice," I admitted. "But he doesn't have it here. He keeps it at his house and brings it with him."

The grass was still saturated with dew, which glistened even in the dim morning light. Droplets of water grabbed hold of my black boots as we made our way around my uncle's cabin. Penny was strutting a little too quickly and I lingered a foot or so behind. Eyeing her pack, I unexpectedly felt underdressed and unprepared.

"What else do you have in that thing?"

"Water. Snacks. The body of Jimmy Hoffa."

"Yeah? The 1990s just called and they want their joke back."

"Not funny," she replied, pretending to pout. "You know that decade is a sore subject for me."

"You weren't even alive then."

"Exactly."

"You seem very prepared, is all I'm saying," I replied. "You said that you've never been hiking before. Were you secretly a Girl Scout when you were little?"

"I dressed up as a slutty Girl Scout for Halloween a couple of years ago. Does that count?"

"Not in any way that matters right now," I replied. "Do you still have the costume? Did you bring it?"

"You wish," she said. "Is that it?"

"Yeah."

My uncle had been right. Tall foliage had nearly overtaken the trail, but a faint outline was still visible. The bordering trees were slowly taking back the path, as well, hugging it so tightly that the head of the trail resembled a dark, shadowy tunnel. For a brief moment, within the darkest of the perceivable shadows, I pictured a pair of glowing orange eyes watching us. I quickly shook the mental image away, but the cold chills were harder to shrug off.

Taking a deep breath, I listened to the early birds singing somewhere in the trees, and it helped to ease my mind. All was fine, as long as the birds were happy. If the music stopped, that's when I would worry.

"According to my uncle, there is a whole system of riding trails that we can use. I guess they go for miles all around the area."

"A system of trails?" Penny asked, pausing. "That sounds confusing. Won't we get lost?"

"No," I replied. "They all lead back to this main trail, which leads right back here to the cabin. And if we do get turned around or confused, my uncle says that no matter where we are, his cabin will always be due west. We follow the trails west and we'll be fine."

"West?"

"West."

"Did you bring a compass?" she asked. "Because that's the one thing that my pack doesn't have. I doubt the GPS on our phones will work in the middle of nowhere."

"We just follow the sun," I said. "It rises in the east and sets in the west. Piece of cake."

"Piece of cake? Can you tell me where the sun is right now?"

My eyes shifted upward, but the sun was being obstructed from view by either the growing cloud cover or the tops of the trees.

"In the sky?"

"No shit," Penny huffed. "It's a good thing that your major is English lit and not meteorology. My woodsman husband won't have any problem finding his way around, let me tell you. Our barefoot, forest family will hunt blindfolded. We will track our prey by listening to the trees and tasting the wind. Just wait and see."

Without another word, she stomped onto the trail. I hastily followed, a million imaginary orange eyes watching my every move.

5

The trees thinned more and more the further we traveled from the cabin, granting us a clearer view of the beautiful valley. And after hiking for 20 minutes or so, we finally took a break at the peak of a wide hill, so that we could admire the scenery stretching out before us.

The vague four-wheeler path cut a line straight down the center of a long meadow of tall grass, which rolled in shallow waves toward a far-off treeline. White and yellow dandelions covered the field, swaying back and forth in a shifting breeze. A cluster of turkeys were gathered close to the path, no more than 30 yards ahead. They strutted and gobbled, unaware of our looming presence. A dense flock of smaller, brown birds swiftly darted from the nearby oak trees, before disappearing into the overgrown meadow, clearly in search of unsuspecting worms. Even though we couldn't see them, we could hear their cackling.

"This will be our home," Penny said in a hushed voice.

"I'm not..." I started, but then realized my mistake. "You're talking about your forest family, again. Huh?"

"You can live here, too, if you want," she replied. "I'm sure my woodsman husband will teach you his manly ways."

"You really know how to beat a joke to death."

"It is one of my better qualities." She shifted her shoulders and lowered her pink pack to the ground. Diving inside, she pulled free two plastic thermoses of water and handed one of them to me. "Are you hungry, yet? I brought trail mix and some other tasty shit."

"No thanks," I answered.

Popping the top of my thermos, I took a long chug and was surprised by how cold the water felt going down my parched throat. On my left, I watched Penny place her water bottle on the grass and then fumble with the side pocket of her camo pack until eventually finding her cell phone.

"Stand right there," she instructed, motioning to a specific spot of grass in front of her, the phone already raised and pointing in that direction.

Following orders, I attempted to smile for the photo, knowing that she cared more about capturing the pretty field than my uncomfortable smirk. Penny snapped a quick picture and then allowed me to return to her side. Raising the thermos to my lips, I was about to take another long, cold drink when something made me pause. The turkeys. Every one of their heads were suddenly raised, as if startled. Their bodies were still as statues and their feathers were visibly puffed out, making them appear larger than before.

"The turkeys look scared," I whispered.

"They probably just hear us."

"We are being quiet," I replied, my voice still low. "And they are looking somewhere else."

A change in the wind forced a disgusting stench into my nose, nearly causing me to puke. Turning my face away, I started inhaling and exhaling through my mouth, but the odor tasted just as bad as it smelled.

"What is that?" Penny cried out, a hand going to her nose. "It smells like roadkill."

"Like roadkill after baking in the sun for a few days," I replied, "and then covered in fresh diarrhea. Oh my god..."

My words were cut short by the sound of 20 or 30 little birds simultaneously taking flight toward the trees, their flapping wings and clattering beaks blending into a chorus of chaos. The babbling turkeys were right behind them, fleeing in the same direction. In a matter of seconds, the field of tall grass had been emptied, leaving Penny and me all alone.

"We must have spooked them," Penny said.

"Yeah," I reluctantly agreed. "Birds are notoriously skittish."

"Are you ready to keep going?" she asked, her mouth barely opening to mumble the words. "I gotta get away from that smell."

Nodding, I handed over my water, and Penny tucked it away alongside her own. She put her phone away too, closed the pack, and then returned it to her shoulders, which was my signal to start walking again.

Making our way along the trail and across the declining field was a tense and silent endeavor, despite us both agreeing that our presence had been what spooked the birds. Without the cover of the woods, I felt exposed and vulnerable. My attention continually darted back and forth scanning the treeline on both sides of us, expecting a pair of glowing orbs to abruptly appear among the trees. Even though the orange eyes never materialized, the sensation of being watched still prickled the hairs on the back of my neck. And it wasn't until we left the field behind that I could finally breathe.

6

Beyond the field, the path continued sloping gradually downward. At some point, the ground around us started getting higher and higher, until we were walking through a narrow groove in the earth, with sheer walls of layered rock on both sides. I reached out my right arm and let my fingertips trace the divisions of gray, black, and brown stone, which were coarse and weathered. When I pulled my hand away, the tips of my fingers were damp with sweat from the dew-covered rocks. Glancing up to the cliff's edge, I wondered whether or not I could scale the 10 or so feet to the top. I was never much of an athlete, so the odds were against my success.

"Tight squeeze," Penny said, pulling me from my thoughts. "Your uncle's four-wheeler must barely get through here. Turn around. Let me get a picture."

I pivoted and placed my back against the jagged cliffside, but then held up a hand to stop her.

"Wait," I blurted. "Leave your phone. Grab the umbrellas. Hurry."

The sound of rushing water had caught my attention a moment before, and I had assumed that a stream or small river was nearby. However, the moving water seemed to be getting closer and closer, making me realize the truth. It was hard rain moving through the valley, and we would be getting dumped on at any moment. If I'd been paying attention to the sky, which had darkened tenfold over the past few minutes, I might have seen it coming.

Penny handed me one of the two blue umbrellas, and we opened them just in time to catch the instantaneous, overwhelming downpour. The large drops of rain felt like shotgun blasts pummeling the top of my umbrella. Strong winds roared through the four-wheeler trail, the stone walls acting as a tunnel, and tried to pull the umbrella handle from my grip. Rushing water gushed from the tops of the cliffs, forming fierce waterfalls that spilled over us.

"Did you happen to pack a canoe in that bag of yours?" I asked.

"Slipped my mind," she replied.

"We can't stay here, then," I said. "This place is going to fill up like a river. And I'm not much of a swimmer."

We broke into a sloppy jog, our footfalls splashing through the deepening puddles. April showers are often a little cold, but the drops of rain felt more like ice pellets against my face, stinging my cheeks, and biting my nose. I immediately regretted not wearing my parka, because my baggy brown hoodie acted like a sponge, absorbing and holding the bitter water. I would have to shed it the first chance that I had, or there would be no way of getting warm again.

Eventually, the four-wheeler trail ascended and returned us to level ground, but the rain continued its frigid cascade. 20 or so yards away, I noticed a dense cluster of elm trees, full leaves covering their branches. I turned and ran toward them, hoping that Penny would follow my lead. Patches of thick mud grabbed at my feet, and I nearly fell several times as I rushed toward the trees. Thankfully, I arrived there in one piece, with Penny on my heels.

The group of trees provided a partial shield against the rain, allowing us to momentarily fold in our umbrellas. It was better than nothing. Penny and I gathered around the trunk of the innermost tree, cold and drenched, yet filled with searing adrenaline. As my breathing began to settle, Penny grabbed my arm and pulled me close, pressing her frosty lips to mine. Our wet bodies came together, and for nearly a minute I forgot about the weather. But then I felt her muscles tense in my arms.

"What is that?" she asked, her body turning away.

"What is what?"

And then I heard it. Blended nearly perfectly with the beating splashes of rain. A crying baby. Somewhere nearby. The sound was long and shrewd, causing my flesh to squirm and crawl. It was impossible. Yet, it was clear and very real.

"What is that?" Penny repeated, visibly shaken.

"Maybe it's a mountain lion," I said.

"That doesn't make me feel any better," Penny replied. "Are there mountain lions in Ohio?"

As the crying transformed into a shrill, infantile howl, that awful stench returned, even worse than before. I peered through the blanket of falling rain, searching for the source of the sound, but all I saw were trees, trees, and more trees.

"Where is it coming from?" Penny asked, her voice barely a whisper.

"I'm not sure," I replied, mine just as quiet. "Sounds like it is coming from over there."

Wiping water from my eyes, I squinted and looked even harder, my sights aimed in the direction I was sure the crying emanated from. A flash of orange caught my attention, but it was there and then instantly gone. The crying baby also stopped just as suddenly, leaving us with only the *pittering, pattering* rain.

For over a minute, neither Penny nor I spoke. In the silence, I listened for the birds, but didn't hear any. Do birds sing in the rain? I couldn't be sure. But the absence of their song was unnerving.

"I've had enough hiking for one day," she said, finally breaking the tension.

"Me too, I…"

My words were cut short by the frenzied screaming of a woman, a pain-stricken wail that was far louder, much closer, and more alarming than the crying baby.

"Someone's out there," Penny said.

"Who? Who is out there?"

"I don't know," she exhaled. "A woman and her baby. And they sound hurt. We need to do something."

"Why would someone bring their baby into the middle of the woods?" I replied, but the distant look on Penny's face told me that she wasn't listening. "That doesn't make any sense."

"We need to do something," she repeated.

"No…"

But I was too slow when I grabbed for her, and Penny was able to slip from beneath the trees and back into the billowing rain. I pulled a deeply rooted sigh from my chest and then hurriedly chased after her.

7

Rain pelted my face again and stung my eyes, making it hard to see. I still held my umbrella, yet never thought to open it. All I could think about was catching Penny. As I pursued her, I continuously wiped away water to clear my sight, but she remained a smudge in my vision, a rushing smear in the distance. Doing my best to keep up, I barrelled nearly blind through the woods, smashing through bushes, breaking thin branches, and crushing any fragile foliage in my way.

I yelled, "Penny! Stop!" but my voice couldn't match the desperation in the woman's wailing.

No. Not a woman. Or a child. It couldn't be. It didn't make sense. Or maybe it made perfect sense. Maybe there was a mother and child lost or hurt, and my girlfriend was running to save them. I spun the thoughts around in my brain and tried to find an angle that would work, but only discovered more questions whichever way I looked at it.

Penny was lighter and faster, but I somehow gained some ground. Putting all of my energy into my legs, I pushed them hard through the mud and undergrowth. I was nearly caught up to her when we both crashed through an unexpected treeline and into another clearing. We both immediately stopped and gawked in bewilderment.

It wasn't like the other field, empty and majestic. It was much smaller in size and circular in shape. Instead of dandelions swaying in the breeze, the area was filled with six-foot tall mounds of long grass, thin branches, and whatever else could be scavenged from the surrounding valley. Nearly a dozen of the bizarre stacks were cluttered haphazard around the center of the clearing. They were coated in a layer of cold rainwater, which created ripples of rising steam, as if the mounds were heated from the inside. The steam gathered and lingered, filling the clearing with a fine cloud of low-hanging fog.

Steam wasn't the only thing wafting from the weird structures.

"Oh my god!" Penny exclaimed, her face contorting in disgust. "I think we found where that smell is coming from."

And she was right. The stench of death and shit assaulted my senses, making it nearly unbearable to breathe through my nose or mouth. My right arm shot to my face, as I attempted to block the odor with a soaked hoodie sleeve. It helped. But not much. A subtle ache suddenly touched the muscles and joints of my body, most likely from the cold and rain. It felt like more than that, though, like an infection had entered into me, like the rotten stench was penetrating my clothes and being absorbed into my skin.

"What the hell is this?" I asked, my words muffled.

Penny noticed my arm and did the same.

"Beavers?" she replied.

"There isn't any river here," I replied.

"Does that matter?"

"I don't know," I replied. "Hold up. Listen."

"What...?" Her question faltered, and then was replaced by an epiphany. "The screaming stopped."

I nodded.

"I think it stopped the moment we got here. What is going on? Wait here."

As I started walking further into the clearing, Penny quickly grabbed a handful of cloth at the back of my sweatshirt. She didn't say anything. She didn't have to. I was scared too. With Penny's hand still gripping my shirt, we slowly moved together toward the nearest mound, fog parting around us.

From a distance, the structures resembled pointless piles of discarded forest, strange but meaningless. As we approached one, I realized how wrong my assumption had been. The mounds were far more than steaming heaps of clutter and accumulation. They were constructs. Each piece of loose grass. Every branch gathered. Each strand of straw used. Had been tightly and purposefully woven together to form what was clearly a hut.

"Beavers couldn't do that," I said, as I walked around to the other side, where there was a visible opening, one wide enough for a large creature to crawl through. "No. Not beavers."

"What then?" Penny asked.

"Something bigger."

I stooped down, wanting to get a look inside, but something startled me before I could.

Clack!

The sound swiftly echoed through the trees and then faded just as fast. It resembled wood smacking against wood, and it was a dull, nearly hollow sound. Even though the origin wasn't clear, I stood up straight and searched the treeline, anyway. But the constant rain and deepening fog made it hard to see anything beyond the clearing, everything along the treeline was masked behind a thin veil of blur and haze.

Swallowing hard, I did my best to calm my overactive imagination. It was a falling tree branch. Or two branches hitting off each other in the wind. That was all. Nothing more.

Clack! Clack! Clack!

There it was again. The crashing of wood against wood. Not a falling limb. Or branch against branch. It was intentional. Someone or something was doing it on purpose. My left hand tightened around the handle of my umbrella and I held it as if it were a weapon.

"There's someone out there," Penny said. She tightly wrapped her arms around my waist and then buried her face between my shoulder blades. "In the trees. Do you see them?"

Clack! Clack! Clack!

The sound became sharper, more aggressive, and I desperately sought out the source.

Clack! Clack! Clack!

And then I saw it, a hulking figure just beyond the treeline, a broad humanoid shadow standing nearly nine feet tall. Was it a person? A very large person?

Clack! Clack! Clack!

That time, the thumping came from the opposite side of the clearing, and I twisted my head around to find it. There was another massive shadow there between the trees, standing just out of focus.

Clack! Clack! Clack!

My mind and my head spun, because the sound was now coming from all around us. We were surrounded. Helpless, I watched the immense figures, their mammoth arms crashing together whatever they were holding, most likely thick branches or slabs of wood. The thumping went on and on, harder and faster, like the beating drums of an antagonizing army.

And then, all at once, our aggressors let loose a cacophony of female crying and baby sobbing, high-pitched wailing that shattered my psyche into a million shards.

I removed my right arm from my face and held it out in front of me, with my palm exposed. My hand trembled, but I still attempted to defy nature. I needed to protect Penny from whatever was out there. However, the banging and crying were far too strong and I buckled beneath their raw force.

Glancing over my shoulder, I noticed that the direction we had come appeared clear. I shouted back to Penny, demanding that she run. In a flight of terror, we fled the clearing. As we rushed for the trees, I fully expected a hulking figure to be hiding there, ready to grab us. Luckily, we broke the treeline unabated and continued running in a direction I hoped would lead back to the four-wheeler trail.

The clacking and wailing ceased the instant we left the clearing, but then the shadows started following us, while remaining just beyond clear visibility. They made zero effort to stay quiet, their enormous bodies pummeling through the woods with the stealth of an elephant stampede. They wanted us to hear them, to know that they were still there.

We found the trees where we kissed, and then found the overgrown trail not far from there. We didn't stop running until we were back at the dandelion field. It was still empty. No gobbling turkeys or flock of little birds. Either they had heard us coming, or they had never returned.

Cautiously, we walked the length of the grassy meadow, fully exposed and helpless. When we reached the middle, I paused, turned, and glanced behind us. A line of shadows stood within the treeline, their orange eyes watching us. They were silent and still, but their intentions were easily understandable. They were letting us leave. But it would be a one-time deal. If we ever came back, things would end differently.

"Are they still there?" Penny asked.

"Yeah," I replied. "But I think we're safe."

The rain wasn't falling as hard, but I still seized the moment to open my umbrella. I gave it to Penny, who was shivering, her lips slightly blue. I then took the other umbrella from her trembling hand and opened it for myself.

"Let's go," I said and got moving again.

As we continued following the four-wheeler trail, the rain lessened more and more, until finally stopping altogether. Pushing our tired, wet bodies, we power walked to my uncle's cabin and immediately packed our stuff. Once the trunk of my car was loaded, we climbed inside and brought the little vehicle to life. After switching on the heat to warm our cold bones, we backed up and pulled away.

Spring break was far from over, but our time in the wilderness was done.

8

The drive back to Columbus was done in contemplative silence, neither one of us sure what to say or how to process what had happened. What were those creatures? Why did they let us go? How long have they been living out there in those grassy huts? Did my uncle ever encounter them? If he did, why hasn't he ever talked about it? A few possibilities nagged at me, but none of them were sane enough to say out loud. If

Penny hadn't been there to see those things too, I would have assumed that I had gone totally mad.

Maybe I had gone mad out there, nothing more than a frantic psycho running around in the pouring rain. Or was being crazy more believable than the alternative? Denial was a happy place, after all.

Penny and I went our separate ways over the next few days, most likely avoiding both each other and the inevitable, uncomfortable conversation. Until I eventually received a text from her asking to meet for lunch. They say you can't read tones in a text message, but her intention was loud and clear. It was time to talk.

She was already seated when I arrived, and I slid wordlessly into the booth across from her. Penny's expression was hard to read, but the dark circles and bags around her eyes screamed volumes. She wasn't sleeping. She was tired. And I was pretty sure that I had those same dark circles and bags around my eyes, as well.

"Penny..." I began, attempting to speak first. But she cut me off by sliding her cell phone across the table. Confused, I looked at her, then at the cell, and then back at her. "What is this? Why are you giving me your phone?"

"Do you remember when we first found the dandelion field?"

I nodded.

"And I took your picture?"

Realization dawned on me like a bright spring morning and I snatched the cell phone from the table. It was already unlocked and opened to Penny's photo gallery, three rows of thumbnails filling the screen. I didn't need to scroll in order to find the picture, because it was the very first tiny image in the very first row. For a couple of seconds, my thumb hovered over the phone screen, unsure whether I was ready. Denial was a happy place, but it was also a lonely one. Taking a breath, I clicked the thumbnail and let the photo fill the screen.

I saw myself, my upper body forever captured like a recent memory, a smirk on my lips, and a thumbs-up presented to the camera. The field stretched out behind me, white and yellow dandelions across an ocean of knee-high grass. Like on that day, the turkeys grabbed my attention, their heads raised in full alert. They were staring wide-eyed toward the treeline on the right. And then I remembered. The picture had been taken moments before both them and the small birds had rushed off into the trees. Initially, Penny and I assumed that our presence had spooked them.

They hadn't been running from us, though.

With my thumb and index finger, I zoomed in on the treeline along the right edge of the photo and gasped.

"Do you see it?" Penny asked.

And I did.

When the picture was taken, the rain hadn't yet begun to fall. There were still small gaps between a few of the gray clouds, and those gaps allowed beams of sunlight to fall through. A hulking figure was stepping into the field, directly into one of those beams. It resembled a large man, walking upright on two muscular legs, two powerful arms swinging by its side. The beast was naked, covered from head-to-toe in long black hair that was filthy and matted. Most of its facial features were buried beneath thick fur and picture blur. Yet, its orange eyes were glowing with intensity as it glared directly at Penny and me.

I handed the phone back, unsure what to say at first.

"It must have ducked back into the trees once it saw us," Penny said, breaking the awkward silence. "Or maybe it had been following us the whole time."

"Yeah," I agreed. "It was so close. How did we not see it?"

"We should go back," she blurted unexpectedly.

"What?" I replied, my mouth gaping. "Why the hell would we do that?"

"Because," she began, the dimple on her cheek deepening, "I think I just found my broad-chested woodsman."

We both laughed for a long time and the tension in my shoulders relaxed. For the first time in a few days, I felt less anxious, less stressed.

"You could braid his hair," I told her. "Your kids won't win any beauty contests, though."

"That's okay," she replied, tucking a strand of golden hair behind her ear. "They will be beautiful to me."

"Did you order?" I asked, picking up the menu sitting in front of me. "I'm starving."

"Not yet."

After summoning the server and placing our orders, Penny steered the conversation in a different, less hairy direction, and I was happy to follow her lead. I would follow her anywhere, I realized. And I would fight any broad-chested, fur covered creature that got in my way.

About the Author

After being brutally mauled by a dog as a toddler, Jackson Arthur grew up with a stutter, which caused him to be socially awkward. Instead of interacting with people, he chose to hide his nose in books, causing him to fall in love with fiction. At an early age, he began reading *Goosebumps* and *Fear Street*, before graduating to more adult novels, like *The Stand* and *The Green Mile*. His love of strange stories blossomed into the desire to creep people out with his own brand of weird tales.

Jackson Arthur currently lives in Ohio with his wife, daughter, mean cat, and old chinchilla.

You can find Jackson Arthur on Facebook by visiting

JacksonArthurStories

Or follow him on Twitter

@Jacksonhorror

His website can be found at:

https://jacksonarthurstori.wixsite.com/website

You can even email him at:

jacksonarthurstories@gmail.com

Made in the USA
Monee, IL
21 April 2022

95153861R00024